Sherman
and
Pearl

Tricia Tusa

Macmillan Publishing Company   New York
Collier Macmillan Publishers   London

Printed and bound in Japan. First American Edition   10   9   8   7   6   5   4   3   2   1

The text of this book is set in 16 point Schneidler Medium.
The illustrations are rendered in pencil and watercolor.

Library of Congress Cataloging-in-Publication Data
Tusa, Tricia. Sherman and Pearl/Tricia Tusa.—1st American ed. p. cm. Summary: An elderly
couple happily spend their days waving to all the passersby on their rural road—until a
freeway is built.
ISBN 0-02-789542-4
[1. Roads—Fiction. 2. Travelers—Fiction.] I. Title. PZ7.T8825Sh 1989   [E]—dc19
88-1630   CIP   AC

To all those at Duchesne,
with heartfelt appreciation

Say hello to Sherman and Pearl.

Sherman and Pearl wave all day,

every day,

to folks who pass by on the road through town…

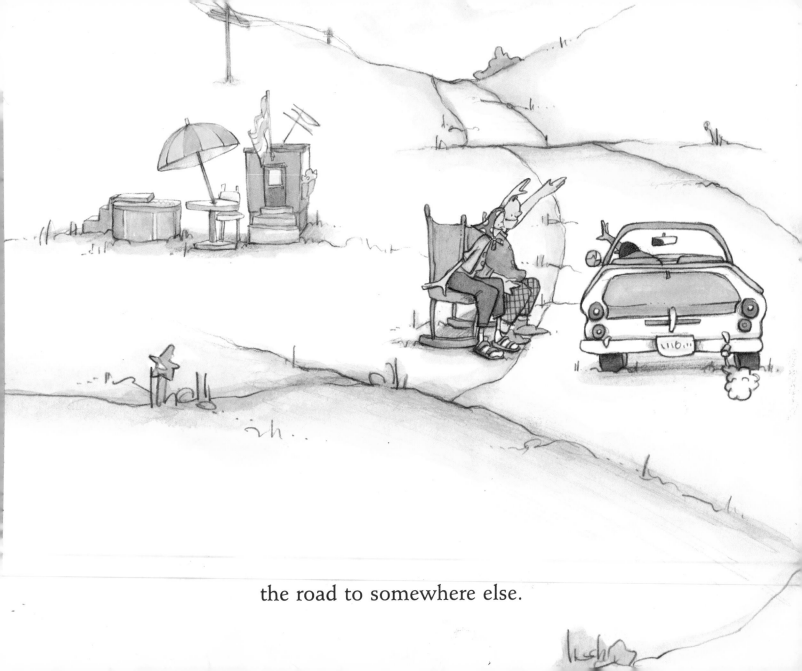

the road to somewhere else.

Some wave back.

Some speed by with their windows shut tight,

or blast their horn.

Some stop and want to know what's wrong.

A few take the time to chat and swap tales.

Some make ugly faces,

or yell out ugly things.

Kids always wave…

except when they go through a certain stage.

Spending their days being friendly makes
Sherman and Pearl very, very happy.

Then, without warning, the bulldozers come,

and up goes a freeway beside the old dirt road.

Being friendly becomes difficult.

Sherman and Pearl become sad.

But they refuse to lose hope.

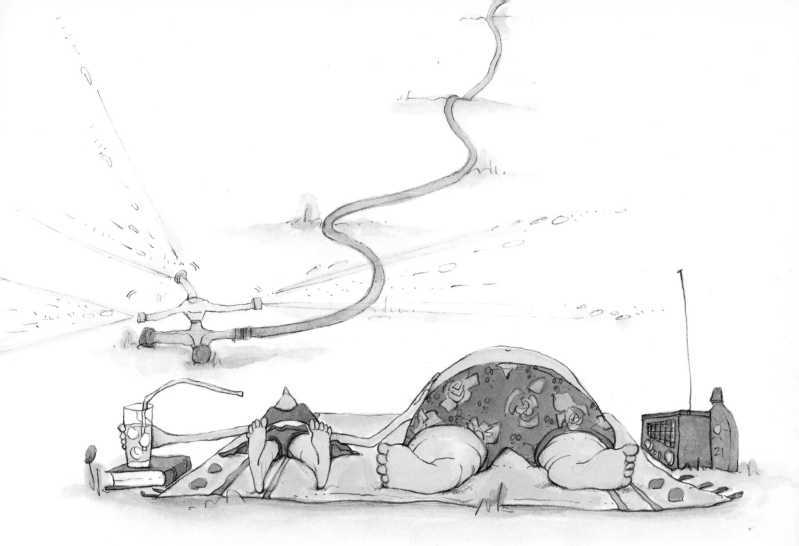

They wait…and wait…and wait some more,

until, sure enough, life returns to the way it was.

Only now *all* who pass by smile and wave
and say hello to Sherman and Pearl.